Estelle and Lucy

by Anna Alter

GREENWILLOW BOOKS

An Imprint of HarperCollins*Publishers*

Estelle and Lucy
Copyright © 2001 by Anna Alter
All rights reserved. Printed in Singapore
by Tien Wah Press.
www.harperchildrens.com

Pen and ink with watercolor were used for the full-color art.
The text type is Korinna.

Library of Congress Cataloging-in-Publication Data

Alter, Anna.
Estelle and Lucy / by Anna Alter.
     p. cm.
"Greenwillow Books."
Summary: Little Lucy wants to do everything Estelle can do,
but Estelle keeps pointing out that Lucy is too small.
ISBN 0-688-17882-0 (trade). ISBN 0-688-17883-9 (lib. bdg.)
[1. Size—Fiction. 2. Cats—Fiction. 3. Mice—Fiction.]
I. Title.   PZ7.A4635 Es 2001   [E]-dc21   00-032113

10 9 8 7 6 5 4 3 2 1
First Edition

FOR BECKY

Estelle's favorite biscuits
are raspberry biscuits.
"Can I help?" asks Lucy.

"Lucy always wants to do what
  I'm doing," says Estelle.
"That's because she wants to be
  big and smart like you," says Mother.

"Like you," says Lucy.

"Well, I am still the biggest,"
says Estelle. "My stirring spoon
is bigger. My mixing bowl is bigger.
Even my chair is bigger."

"Please bring your bowl to the kitchen,"
says Mother. "I will add your dough
to mine."
"Lucy's spoon is too small to stir,"
says Estelle. "Her bowl is too
small to mix. Even her chair is
too small for the table. . . ."

"I can reach the countertop
all by myself," says Estelle.

"I can climb the stepstool
and make a shadow as big
as a house.

"I am big enough to fit in
Papa's slippers and *slip-slop*
down the long front hall.

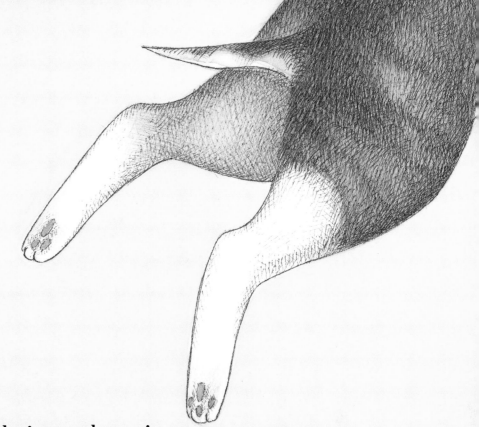

"I can jump up high into the air . . .

"and run to the porch
like a lightning bolt.

"I can even swing on the
high, skinny swing!

"Lucy is too small for those things.
She is too small for many things.
She only fits in the swing for babies."

"I think Lucy is just the right size for a picnic," says Mother. "Will there be raspberry biscuits?" asks Estelle.

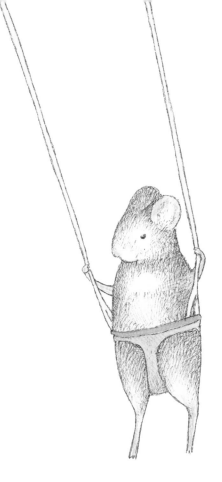

"Yes," says Mother.
"Big ones and little ones."